D0211614

THE DARK KNIGHT™

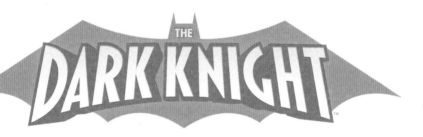

SUPER DC HEROES

THE DARK KNIGHT

BATMAN AND THE KILLER CROC OF DOOM!

WRITTEN BY
LAURIE S. SUTTON

ILLUSTRATED BY
LUCIANO VECCHIO

BATMAN CREATED BY BOB KANE

STONE ARCH BOOKS
a capstone imprint

PUBLISHED BY STONE ARCH BOOKS IN 2012
A CAPSTONE IMPRINT
1710 ROE CREST DRIVE
NORTH MANKATO, MN 56003
WWW.CAPSTONEPUB.COM

CATALOGING-IN-PUBLICATION DATA IS AVAILABLE AT THE
LIBRARY OF CONGRESS WEBSITE.

ISBN: 978-1-4342-4097-2 (LIBRARY BINDING)
ISBN: 978-1-4342-4215-0 (PAPERBACK)

SUMMARY: WHEN DOZENS OF GOTHAM CITIZENS ARE
KIDNAPPED, THE DARK KNIGHT JUMPS INTO ACTION. SEVERAL
CLUES LEAD TO THE SEWERS, WHERE HE FINDS AN ARMY OF
HALF-HUMAN, HALF-CROCODILE ZOMBIES AND THEIR LEADER,
KILLER CROC! AND WHEN BATMAN IS INFECTED, HE'LL NEED
TO FIND A CURE OR BECOME ANOTHER ONE OF CROC'S
REPTILIAN WARRIORS.

ART DIRECTOR: BOB LENTZ
DESIGNER: BRANN GARVEY

PRINTED IN THE UNITED STATES OF AMERICA
IN STEVENS POINT, WISCONSIN.
042013   007349R

TABLE OF CONTENTS

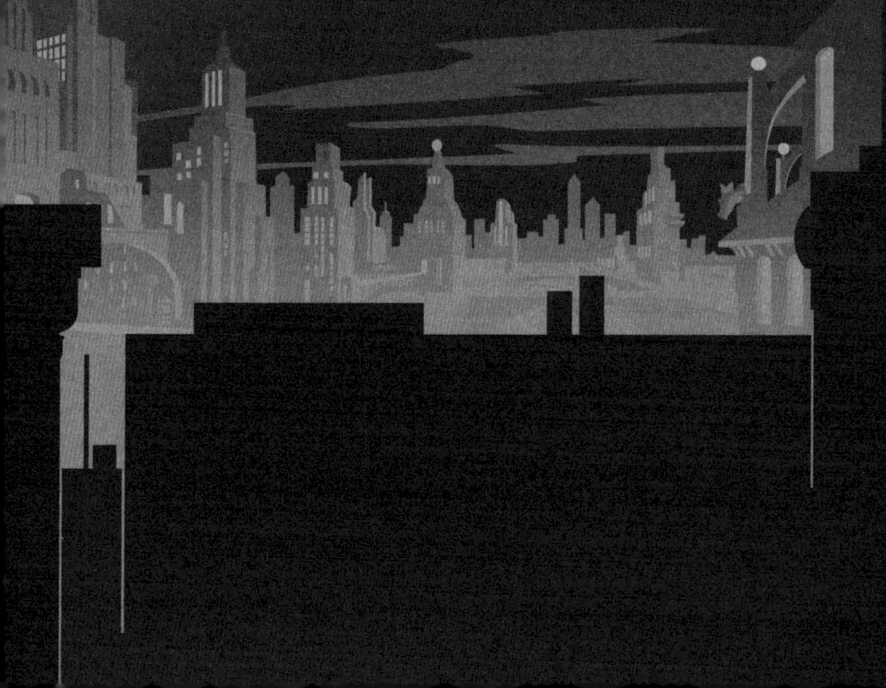

WHILE STILL A BOY, BRUCE WAYNE WITNESSED THE BRUTAL MURDER OF HIS PARENTS. THE TRAGIC EVENT CHANGED THE YOUNG BILLIONAIRE FOREVER. BRUCE VOWED TO RID GOTHAM CITY OF EVIL AND KEEP ITS PEOPLE SAFE FROM CRIME. AFTER YEARS OF TRAINING HIS BODY AND MIND, HE DONNED A NEW UNIFORM AND A NEW IDENTITY.

HE BECAME...

THE
DARK KNIGHT
™

CHAPTER 1

THE CROC STRIKES MIDNIGHT

The roar of motorcycle engines echoed down the midnight streets of Gotham City. A gang of riders traveled in a loose pack, ignoring the speed limit and running every red light. They were dressed in black leather jackets and ragged jeans. No one wore a helmet — they laughed at danger and at the law.

Their leader was a man who looked more like a reptile than a human. His skin was green and scaly. He had no hair on his head, just two rows of rigid bumps.

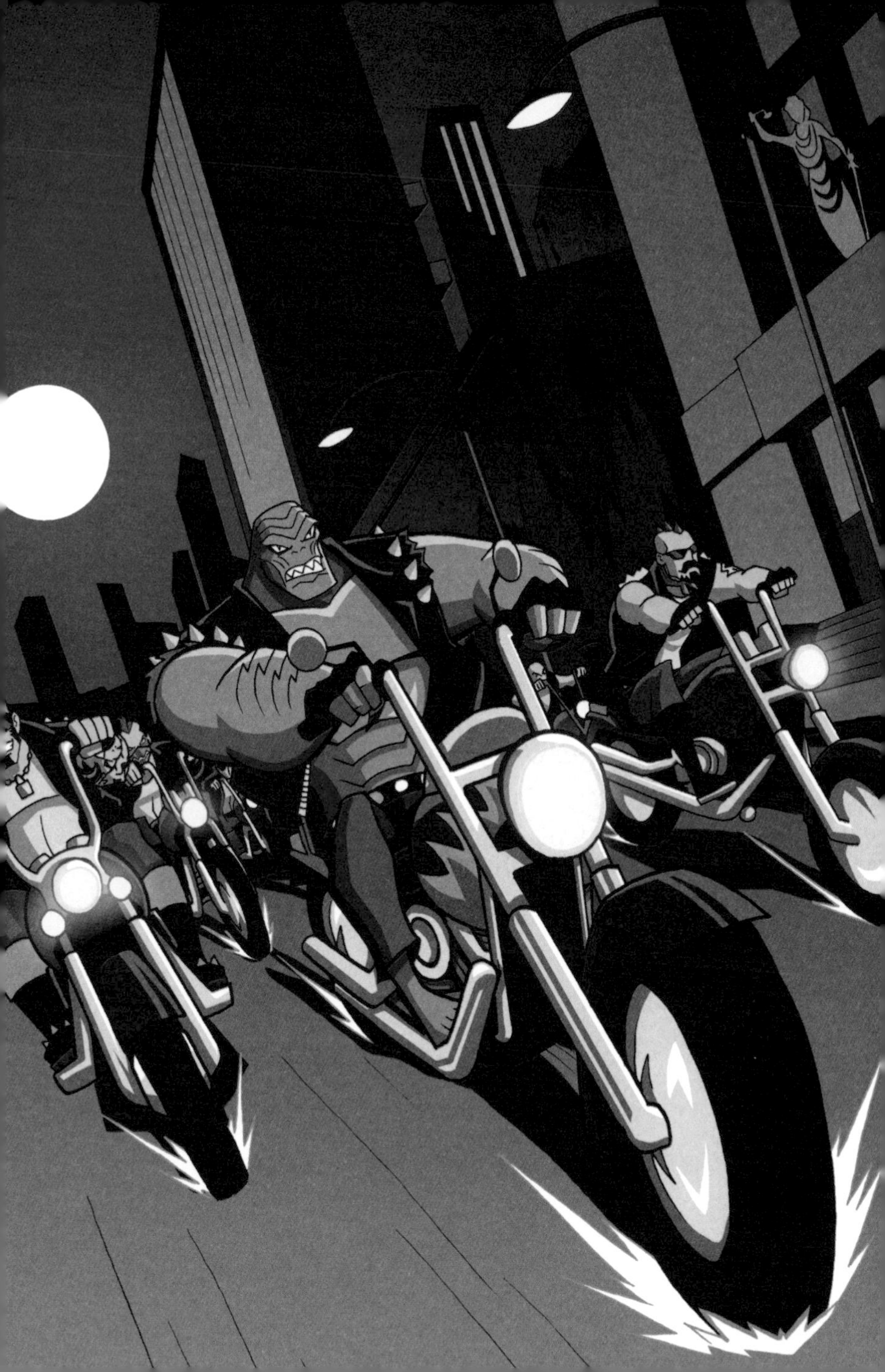

Boots did not fit over his giant feet, so he always went barefoot. He gripped the motorcycle's handlebars with his strong, claw-like hands.

He was Killer Croc.

The villain had been born with a disease that deformed his skin and limbs. His family had abandoned him because of it. He did not remember much about them except for their disgust. Growing up, he didn't have any friends because of his freakish appearance. Not that he knew what friendship was, really. All his life he had been despised. All his life he had been an outsider.

"Alley-Gators, follow me!" Killer Croc commanded his gang. He steered his motorcycle into Gotham Park. The other riders followed.

The motors on the big bikes rumbled as the gang made its way deeper into the forest refuge. The sound awoke the people sleeping there. Frightened birds took flight. Scared squirrels scampered to higher branches. A group of homeless people huddled closer together for protection.

Killer Croc and his Alley-Gator gang stopped their motorcycles in front of the huddling, frightened people. These were Gotham City's most vulnerable citizens. That's why they were easy prey.

"Look at what we have here," Killer Croc said. "Fresh meat."

The villain leaned over and bared his sharp teeth at the cowering people. His boney jaws looked skeletal. Killer Croc hissed at his shivering victims like a snake. One of the homeless men let out a shriek.

Killer Croc sneered at the man. "You're pathetic," he said. It was the same thing Killer Croc had been told his whole life. Turning the tables made Killer Croc feel superior.

Killer Croc jumped off his motorcycle and shoved the man. The man fell backward into his companions, making them all tumble into a heap on the wet grass. They all looked up in fear at the giant before them. They were too afraid to even stand.

The Alley-Gators surrounded the helpless victims. One of the men looked up at the attackers with fear on his face. Then he saw something else. His expression changed to hope. He actually smiled.

"What are you grinning at?" one of the gang members snarled.

POW! Something slammed into the thug. The Alley-Gator was thrown into the other gang members. They stumbled and rolled over each other on the slippery ground. Killer Croc was caught up in the tangle and landed face-first in a puddle.

"Spffftt! Pteeew!" he said, spitting mud out of his mouth. "Clumsy idiots! What are you —?"

A large shadow moved close to Killer Croc in the darkness. A chill ran down the villain's spine. He couldn't help feeling a dagger of fear stab the most primitive part of his brain. His worst nightmare was standing over him.

"Batman!" the crook cried out.

"I see you've sunk to a new low, Killer Croc," the Dark Knight said.

Killer Croc didn't answer. His voice was caught in his throat. Batman scared him, and Killer Croc hated being scared. It made him angry.

"Your career as a super-villain was never something to boast about," Batman said. "But harassing homeless people? That's pretty low, even for you."

It made Killer Croc even angrier to be reminded that his criminal career was a joke. None of the super-villains of Gotham City took him seriously. Even in a society of super-freaks like the Penguin, Two-Face, and the Joker, Killer Croc got no respect.

"I'm taking you off the streets and putting you in a jail cell," Batman told Killer Croc. "And your motorcycle pals are coming with you."

The thought of being penned up again was the last straw. Killer Croc's rage boiled and swelled, driving him into action. "You're not caging me like an animal in a zoo!" he bellowed.

Killer Croc lashed out with his clawed hands and slashed Batman across the chest. *RIPPPPPPPPPPPPPPPPP!* The Dark Knight was caught by surprise and jumped back by instinct. The fabric of his uniform was shredded.

"You're fast, I'll give you that," Batman said, unharmed. "But you're still no better than a common bully."

The Dark Knight used his words just like any of the weapons in his Utility Belt. He knew what he said would make Killer Croc angry. He knew his enemy was insecure and ashamed of himself.

Batman's goal was to make Killer Croc angry, to let the villain's emotions get the best of him.

ROOOOARRRR! Killer Croc didn't think at all. He lunged at the Dark Knight. Batman sidestepped Killer Croc's blind rush. Then he used his opponent's own speed against him by tripping him and directing him straight toward a thick tree trunk. *THUD!*

"Did that knock any sense into you?" Batman asked.

Killer Croc staggered to his feet. He swiped wildly at the Dark Knight with his claws. Batman easily evaded the angry, predictable attacks.

"I guess not," Batman said, answering his own question. "Let's wrap this up."

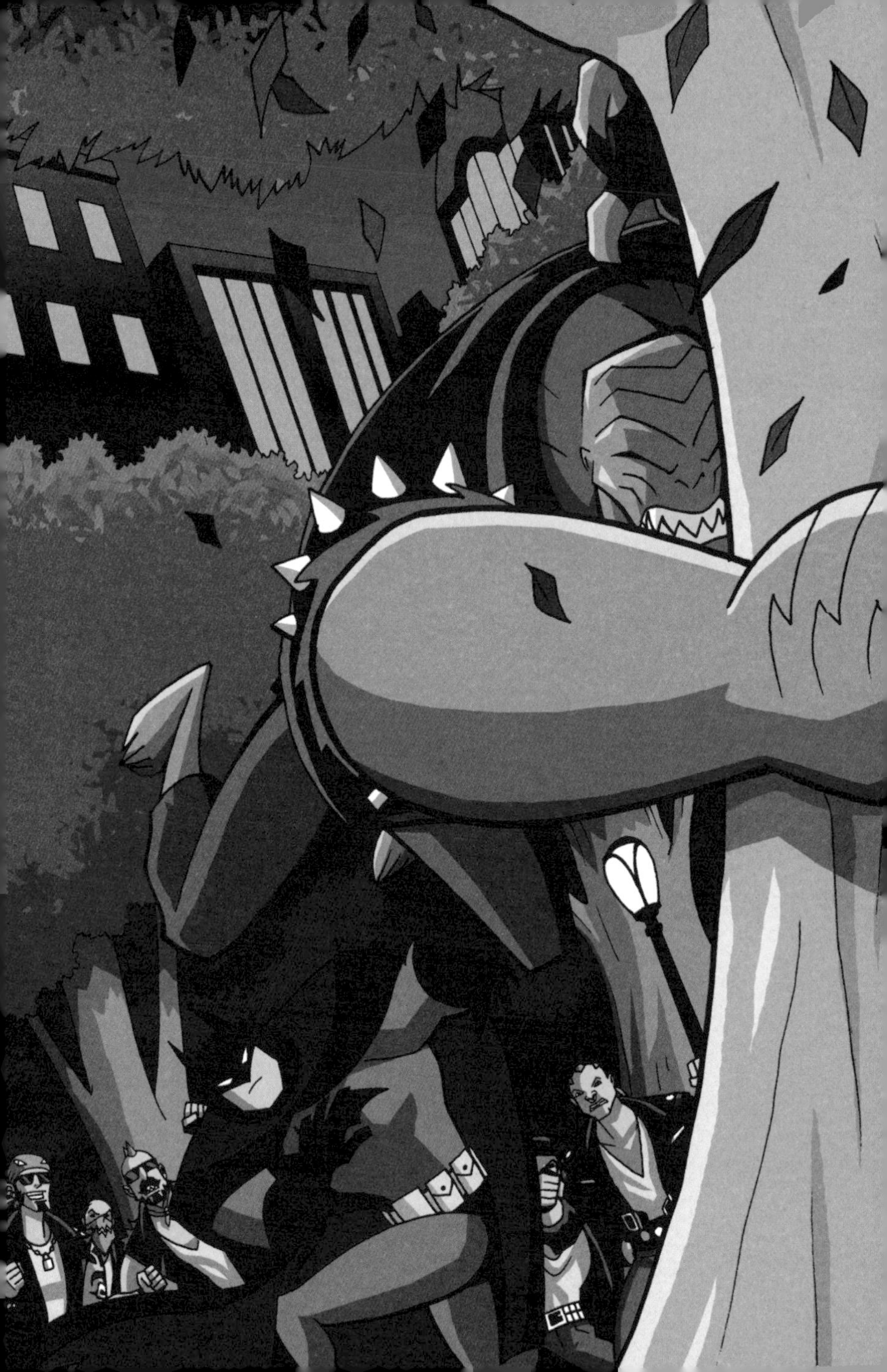

The Dark Knight pulled a Batrope from his Utility Belt. He was about to use it to snare Killer Croc when a cloud of smoke erupted at his feet. *POOF!* Suddenly, he was as blind as a bat. Batman reached for a gas mask from his Utility Belt. *SCHING!* Something sharp cut through the belt, making it drop to the ground.

Batman was forced to retreat from the smoke. When he reached clear air he looked back to where he'd been. A thin fog was all that was left. There was no sign of Killer Croc or the Alley-Gators. They had all escaped.

One of the gang members must have used a smoke bomb, Batman thought.

The Dark Knight left to search for the homeless men to make sure they were safe.

Batman didn't see the dark shape of a tall man watching him from the shadows. When Batman left, the shape turned and walked to where Killer Croc sat behind some bushes. The strange man held out his hand to the reptilian villain.

"Come with me if you want to defeat Batman," the stranger said.

Killer Croc looked up at the man, but his eyes were blurry and stinging from the smoke. All he could see was a dark shape in the night.

"Did you throw that smoke bomb?" Killer Croc asked, rubbing his eyes.

"Yes," the shadow answered.

"Why?" Killer Croc asked.

"I have my reasons," was the man's mysterious reply.

Killer Croc narrowed his eyes at the man, but said nothing.

"I repeat," said the strange man, "come with me if you want to defeat the Dark Knight."

Killer Croc didn't know this person or his plan, but since he wanted to destroy Batman, Killer Croc was okay with that. He stood up and shook the man's hand.

"It's a deal," Killer Croc agreed with a sinister smile. His jagged teeth glittered in the moonlight. "Let's take a bite out of Batman."

CHAPTER 2

KILLER CROC HUNTER

A few days later, Batman stood with Police Commissioner James Gordon on the roof of police headquarters. Gordon had called the Dark Knight for a special meeting. They were alone, with only the full moon looking down on them.

"Something strange is going on," Gordon said. "Strange even for Gotham City."

"What can I do to help?" Batman asked.

"It's a missing persons case," Gordon said. "Actually, it's several missing persons cases."

"What do you mean?" Batman asked.

"Every homeless person in Gotham Park is missing," Gordon explained.

"All of them?" Batman asked.

"The entire population is gone. That's a total of a hundred citizens," Gordon replied.

"Is it possible they just moved to a different location or left town?" Batman asked.

"No, they've just disappeared," Gordon replied. "It's a real mystery."

Batman smiled. "Mysteries are my specialty," said the World's Greatest Detective.

Ten minutes later, Batman was looking for clues in Gotham Park where he had fought Killer Croc and his gang.

Killer Croc had not been seen since that night, making Batman wonder if the scaly super-villain might be behind the disappearances.

The Dark Knight took a small device out of his Utility Belt. It looked like a flashlight, but the beam was special. It would pick up any trace of chemicals on the ground. Batman's theory was that the homeless people had been knocked out by a gas grenade and kidnapped. That would've been the quickest way to take them by surprise.

BEEEP! BEEEP! The little device in Batman's hand alerted him to small amounts of an unusual substance. A tiny monitor displayed its chemical formula.

"I was right," Batman said to himself. "Someone used knock-out gas, and it's a very unusual compound."

The Dark Knight took a pair of high-tech goggles from his Utility Belt and strapped them over his eyes. Now he could see where the grass had been crushed under the weight of many human bodies. He could also see where the bodies had been dragged. Batman carefully followed the faint trail.

Batman couldn't blame the Gotham City Police for missing the evidence. They didn't have the special detection equipment he had invented. They didn't have anything like his Utility Belt. And they definitely didn't have Bruce Wayne's resources.

"The trail leads into the sewers," Batman said. He stood in front of a large storm drain. "This is one of Killer Croc's favorite hangouts. He must be the one behind the disappearances."

Batman took a tiny cutting torch from his Utility Belt. *HISSSSSSS!* He used the device to slice open the metal grate covering the drain tunnel.

He stepped inside and walked down the sloping concrete ledge. Moments later, he entered an underground world.

There was no light in the tunnel. The walls were covered in moss and other strange vegetation. A trickle of smelly rainwater ran beneath Batman's feet. His boots sloshed in the soggy ooze.

Batman walked deeper into the sewers. Numerous drain tunnels branched and split in different directions, but the hero used his high-powered goggles to follow the trail. He could see footprints in the muck and claw marks on the walls. He could smell decay and refuse everywhere.

Suddenly, Batman heard the sound of something moving. *SPLOOOSH! SPLASH!* Something big was moving away in the dark. Even with his special goggles on, Batman couldn't see where or what it was. *HUFF! HUFFFFFF!* The thing's breath was loud — and definitely not human.

Batman recalled stories he'd heard when he was a kid about people releasing baby alligators into the sewers. The little gators grew up to be big gators underneath Gotham City. It was a scary and fun story when he was young, but now he was tracking a real Killer Croc.

Suddenly, a heavy body slammed into the Dark Knight from behind. *THUD!*

An ordinary person would have landed on his face in the foul water.

But the Dark Knight was anything but ordinary. Instead, he tucked into a ball and rolled onto his back. Immediately, he sprang back to his feet. His foe was the one that ended up with a mouth full of muck.

Batman tried to get a glimpse of his attacker, but the hero's tracking goggles had been partially knocked off. If he lost them, he would be blind down here. The Dark Knight reached to readjust them. In that brief moment, his attacker struck a second blow. **WHOMP!** This time, Batman was smashed against the slick sewer wall.

A giant, scale-covered tail swept past his field of vision, but Batman was able to dodge just before it hit him. The cement wall cracked under the impact of the attacker's blow.

CRUNNNNCH!

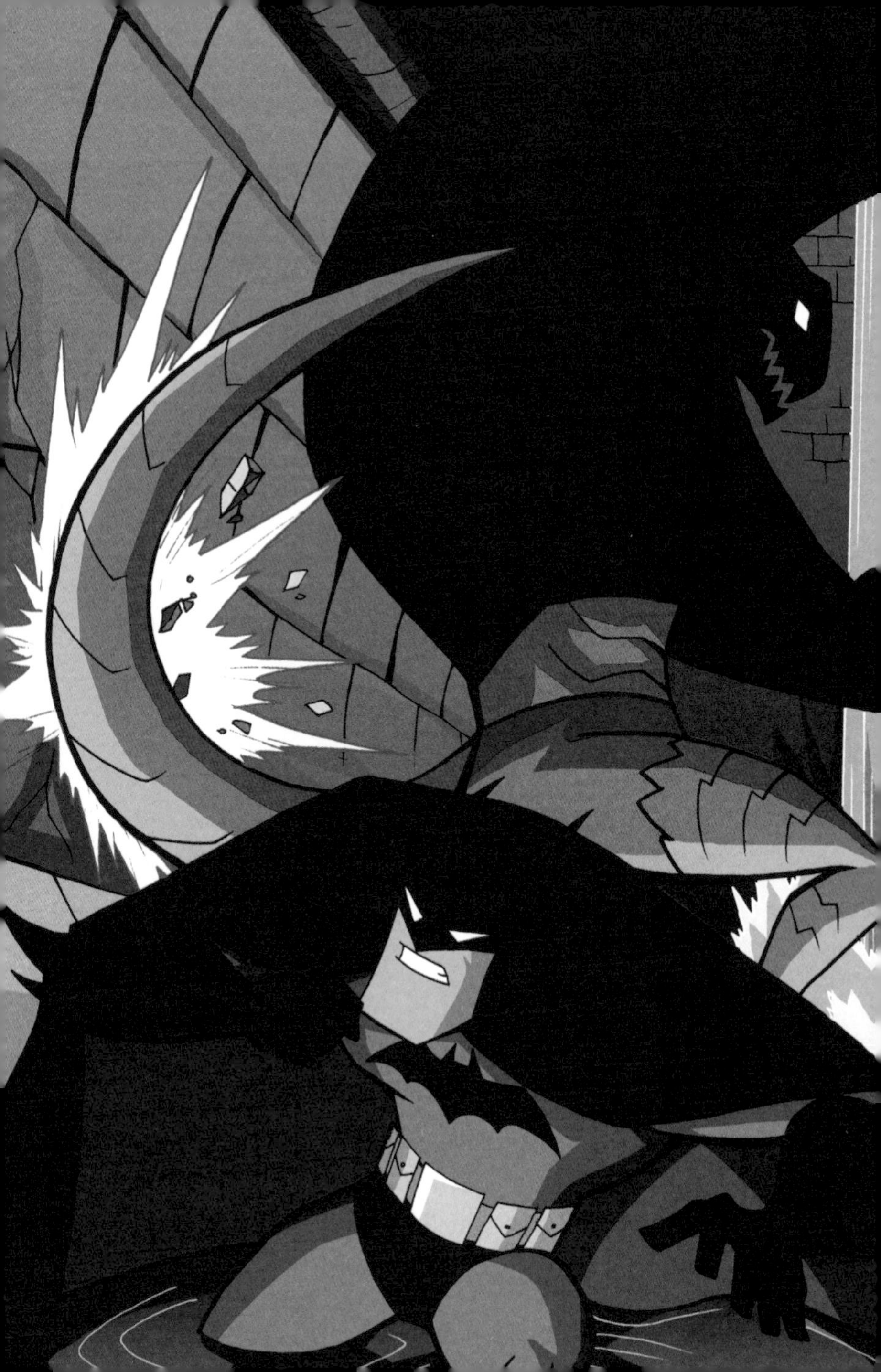

The Dark Knight jumped to his feet, ready to fight back. It took a lot to worry Batman, but the ferocity, size, and strength of his attacker had the Dark Knight on edge.

The Dark Knight glanced around in the dark hoping to catch sight of his opponent. He assumed it was Killer Croc. *But this monster has a tail,* he realized. *Something's not right.*

HIISSSSSS! The monster was right next to his face. Batman twisted to the side. Claws raked the concrete. *SCRAPE!* The Dark Knight reached into his Utility Belt and pulled out a capsule of knockout gas. The creature lunged at him, and Batman cracked the capsule over its snout.

"Not more gas!" the attacker cried. Then he turned and ran.

"That sounded like Killer Croc's voice," Batman said to himself. "But the creature I saw sure didn't look like him."

Batman dashed after his fleeing foe through the filthy sewer tunnel. If it really was Killer Croc he was chasing, then what had happened to him? The attacker looked more like a crocodile than a human.

The sewer was a maze. Sections had been built, abandoned, and rebuilt over the years. There was no map that was accurate. A person — or an alligator — could live down here and no one would ever know about it.

Batman saw a faint light in the distance. Even with his special goggles, the light was very weak. There was only one reason there would be light this far into the maze: it had to be a secret hideout.

Whatever is living down here, Batman thought, *that has to be its home.*

The Dark Knight took off the goggles and let his eyes slowly adjust. He could hear people mumbling somewhere nearby. Then he heard moaning. That meant there were people down here who were suffering or in trouble. They needed his help!

Batman rushed toward the light. He surged into a large chamber where several sewer tunnels met. He spotted his attacker standing in the middle of the room.

The creature stood like a man and had arms and legs shaped like a human's. But that's where its human appearance ended. The beast had a tail and sharp claws like a crocodile. Its snout and teeth were long, jagged, and sharp. Its eyes were savage and beady.

"Waylon, is that you?" Batman asked. He used Killer Croc's real name, hoping to reach the human deep inside the monster.

"Waylon's dead and gone," Killer Croc replied. "How do you like the looks of the new me?"

"What happened?" Batman wanted to know.

"I got a face lift," Killer Croc said with a beastly laugh.

"Who did this to you?" Batman asked. He knew that Killer Croc's monstrous transformation was beyond his own abilities.

"It was my choice, Batman," Killer Croc said with a snarl. "Now I really am a Killer Croc!"

CRAAAAAAAAAACK!

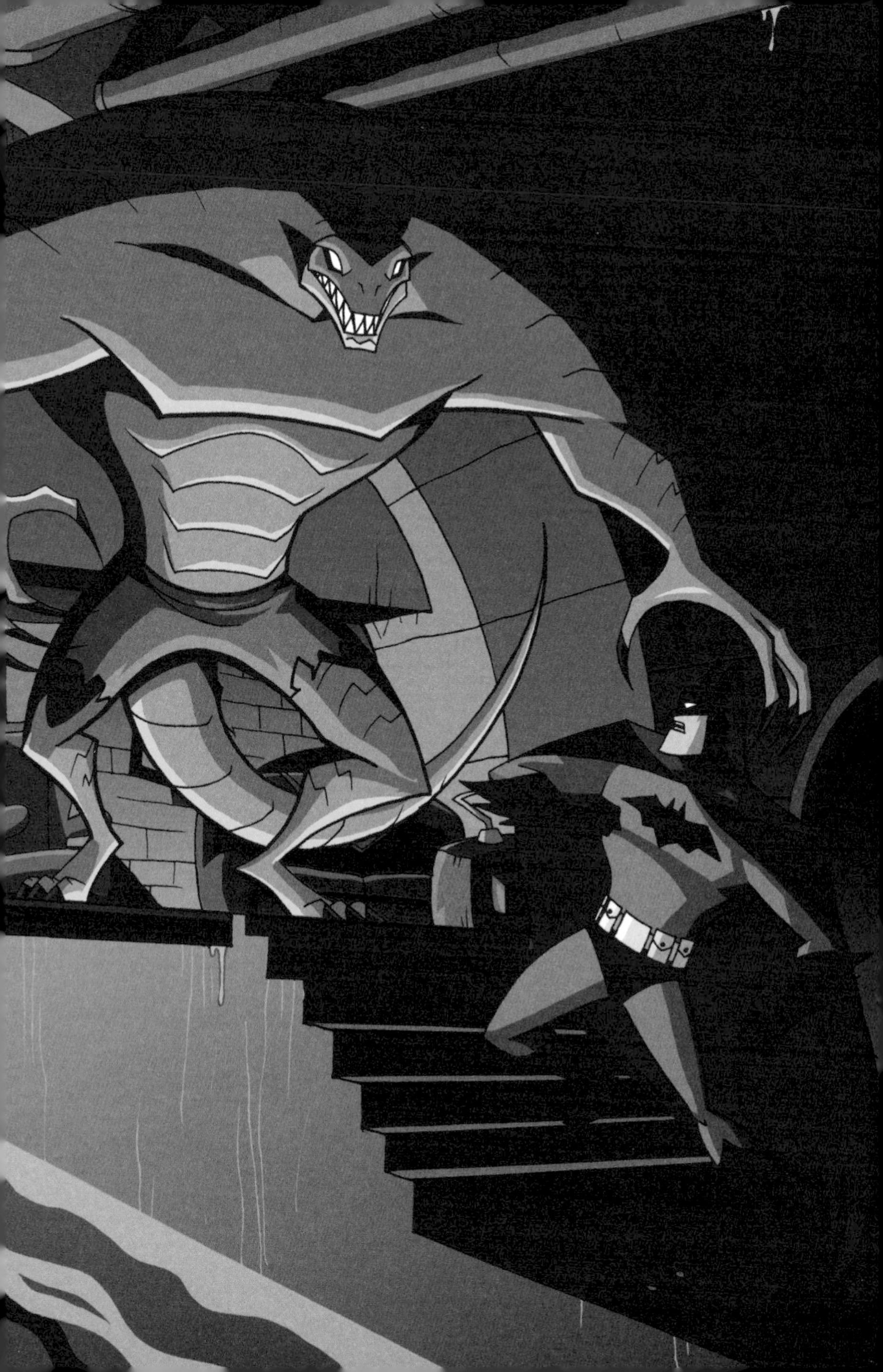

The mutated villain snapped his tail at Batman like a whip. The Dark Knight jumped back just in time to see the tail smash into — and through — a concrete pillar. *CRUNNNCH!* Debris flew everywhere.

In the chaos, a mob of reptile men grabbed Batman. They wrapped their scaly green arms around the Dark Knight and tore at him with claw-like hands. They gnashed at his limbs in mindless hunger, their teeth snapping open and shut like crocodiles. Batman used every bit of strength he had to throw them off, but they kept throwing themselves against the Dark Knight.

As Batman struggled against the reptile men, a small TV camera on the ceiling of the chamber recorded the fight. It panned left and right to follow the action.

The camera was sending a signal to a secret lab far above the sewers where a man watched the action on a giant monitor. It was the same man who had offered to help Killer Croc.

The shadowy villain smiled. "My plan is working perfectly," he said.

CHAPTER 3

ADDED INCENTIVE

The Dark Knight staggered out of the sewer tunnel. Slowly and painfully he made his way back into Gotham Park. He didn't like to retreat, but there were far too many reptile men to fight at once. The Dark Knight had to hand it to Killer Croc — the villain had managed to lure him into a trap.

"At least now I know where all the homeless people went," Batman said to himself. "They were turned into Killer Croc's mutated minions."

But the Dark Knight didn't get any satisfaction from solving that mystery. Someone had used the homeless victims like lab rats in an evil experiment. He didn't know who was behind those terrible mutations, but he was determined to find out.

*   *   *

Batman returned to his crime lab in the Batcave under Wayne Manor. He had technology there that didn't exist anywhere else on the planet. Batman planned to use it to find out who was changing innocent citizens into Killer Croc's monsters.

"I say, sir, what is that, um, intense odor?" Alfred Pennyworth asked when Batman entered the cave.

"I had a little encounter this evening," Batman replied.

The loyal butler sniffed and then grimaced. "With what, sir?" he asked. "A swarm of wet rats?"

"Just some mutated croc people," Batman said.

"Interesting," Alfred said dryly. He offered a wash bin and cloth. "Would you like some hot water and a towel?"

"No thanks," Batman said. "I need the residue for evidence." He took off the cowl of his uniform. "The creatures left plenty of saliva behind for examination."

"May I assist you in any way, sir?" Alfred asked.

"Yes, put this in the DNA sampler, please," Batman said. He held out the damp uniform toward Alfred. "I need to set up the computer for analysis."

"Of course, sir," Alfred said without hesitation. This wasn't the first time he'd been asked to handle evidence. He never faltered, despite any risks involved.

Alfred pulled a pair of latex gloves from his pocket and put them on. Then he took the gooey fabric between two fingers and went to the DNA sampler. The fabric landed on the glass plate with a wet **PLOP!** When he turned around he saw something that worried him.

"Master Bruce, you've been wounded," Alfred said.

"Nothing new about that," Batman muttered. He didn't look up from his work.

"You really need to be more careful, Master Bruce," Alfred said. "I'll get the antiseptic."

Alfred had taken care of Bruce Wayne for a long time. Bruce had been a child when his parents had been killed. Alfred had looked after him since. Bruce had trained for years to avenge his parents' deaths. Alfred had been with him then, too. When Bruce had become Batman in order to fight crime and corruption in Gotham City, Alfred stood by him. He alone knew the Dark Knight's true identity.

"Sir, there's something wrong," Alfred said. His voice was full of concern.

Batman stopped what he was doing. "What is it?" he asked.

"It's your shoulder, sir," Alfred said. "It appears to be . . . growing scales."

Batman looked down at his shoulder. The skin was turning green and scaly before his eyes.

"This looks just like the mutation that's affecting the croc's minions," Batman said in a detached tone. "Their bites must have infected me."

He swabbed his shoulder for a sample and then handed it to Alfred. The loyal butler changed out his latex gloves before he took the swab and put it on another glass panel.

"This is good," Batman said. "Now I'll have DNA from two sources — the croc mutants and me."

"Good?" Alfred protested. "You're infected!"

"Think of it as an incentive to find the antidote," Batman replied with a grin. "If I don't find a cure for those who were turned into reptiles, I won't find a cure for me."

"That does not make me feel better, sir," Alfred replied.

The Dark Knight went to work. His concentration blocked out everything else. Alfred worked next to him, silent and focused.

*   *   *

Killer Croc was inspired by his encounter with Batman. He had forced the Dark Knight to retreat. For once, he had won, and this made him very happy.

Killer Croc led his gang of reptilian men out of the sewers like a general leading an army — a very strange army. The croc mutants half-walked and half-crawled along behind their master. None of them could talk, but they snapped their jaws and clacked their teeth.

They didn't think for themselves, either. They followed Killer Croc just because he told them to.

By now, the sun was just appearing over the horizon. Gotham City was waking up to a new day. So it was a big surprise for the morning commuters to see a horde of reptilian monsters shambling down the street.

However, the strange visitors were no surprise to Commissioner Gordon. Batman had called him and told him everything about the fate of the missing people. Gordon was already waiting at the scene with a squad of police officers and animal control agents.

"I'm not afraid of you," Killer Croc bellowed when he saw the police. "But you're going to be afraid of me!"

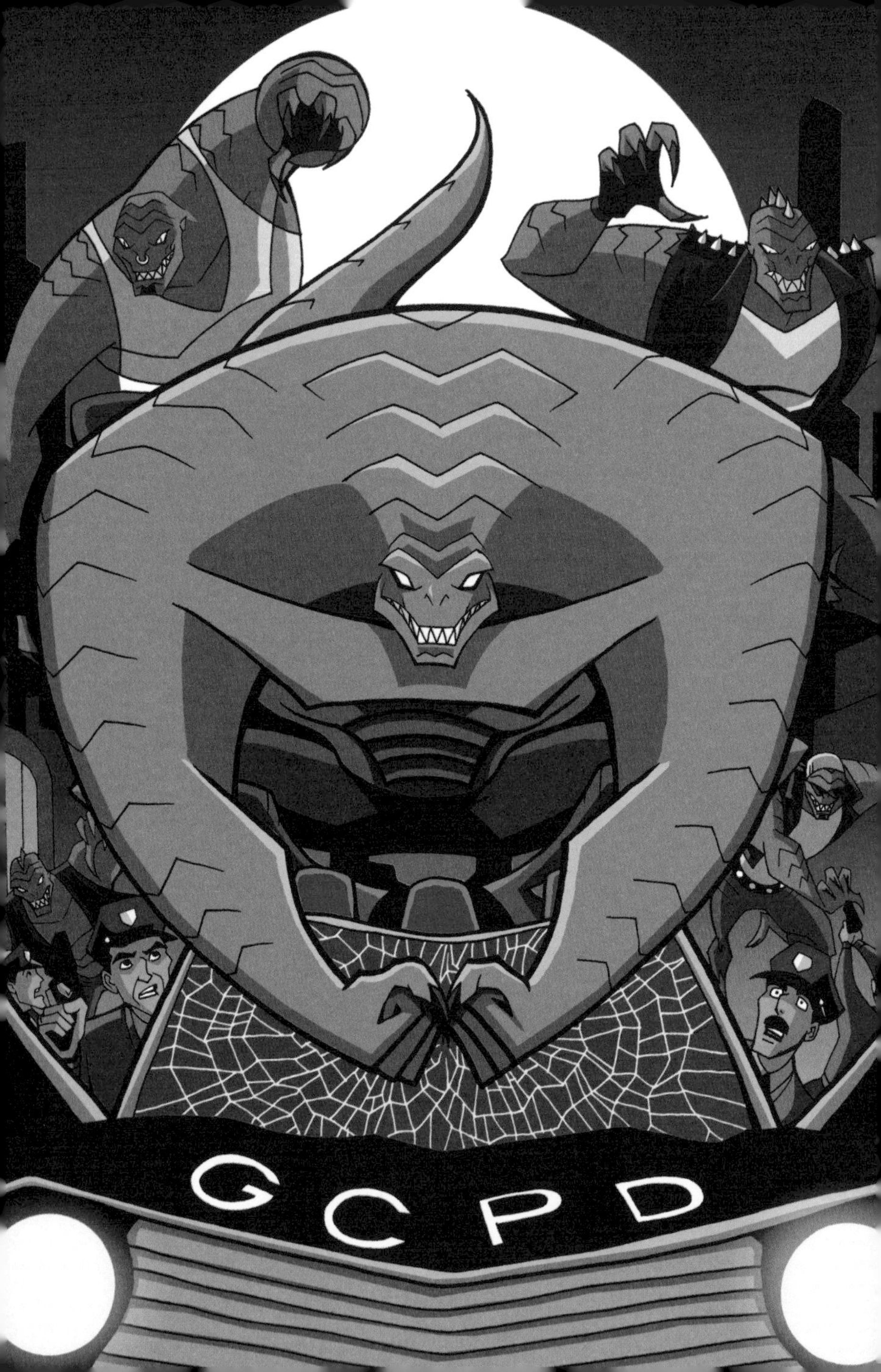
GCPD

Killer Croc jumped onto the hood of the nearest patrol car. The metal dented under his weight. **WHAM!** Killer Croc smashed his fists into the windshield and shattered it.

HAHAHAHAHAHA!

He really loved his improved strength, and he'd been anxious to use it again.

Killer Croc's army swarmed over the other squad cars like a mindless wave. They attacked the officers with their sharp claws and jagged teeth.

"Use the tranquilizer darts!" Gordon ordered. He knew these were innocent people and didn't want his men to shoot them with bullets.

PFFFFT! PFFFFT! The animal control agents fired the special darts. The needles bounced off the reptilian skin.

They were unable to penetrate the thick, protective scales covering their bodies. The croc people continued to rush against the police officers and animal control agents.

"All units fall back!" Gordon ordered. "It's time for Operation Crybaby!"

Killer Croc watched the police retreat. He laughed in triumph, enjoying the sight of men running in fear from his power. He was enjoying himself so much that he almost didn't notice the sound of a helicopter.

Killer Croc looked up just in time to see tear gas canisters drop from above. Clouds of stinging smoke spewed from the cans.

"More gas?" Killer Croc grumbled.

This time he didn't care. The tear gas billowed around him and his reptile army.

HAHAHAHAHA! They laughed at the police's efforts. None of them were affected by the gas.

"Operation Cry Baby is a no-go!" Gordon yelled to his officers and agents. "All forces retreat!"

Suddenly, one of the croc people slammed into Commissioner Gordon. Claws raked his skin and jaws closed around his arm. Gordon kicked the creature away. The mindless reptile man barely flinched.

At that moment, someone pulled the croc minion off of him. When he looked up, he saw Batman! Before Gordon could say a word of thanks, the Dark Knight grabbed him. They zipped up a Batrope to safety, landing on a nearby roof.

"Thanks for the save, old friend," Gordon said.

"I'm afraid it's only temporary," Batman replied. "You've been bitten, Gordon. You're infected."

Gordon looked down at his arm. The skin was starting to turn green and scaly. Then Gordon looked at Batman. The Dark Knight's skin was the same. The part of the hero's face that Gordon could see was covered with scales.

Gordon's eyes went wide. "You too?" he asked.

The Dark Knight nodded.

"This is bad," Gordon said.

"Just more incentive for me," Batman replied.

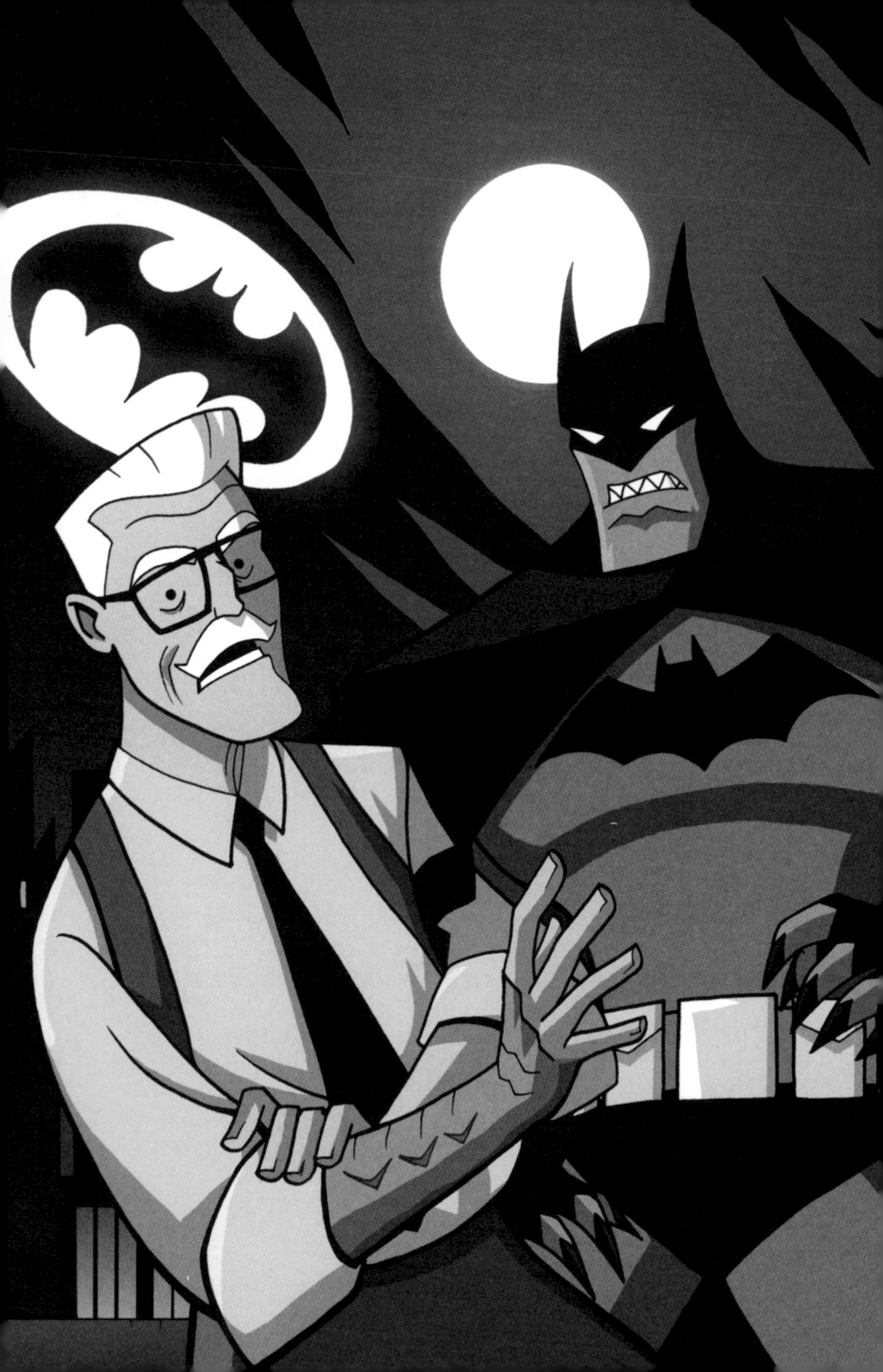

CHAPTER 4

CROOKED CROCS

By noon, the infection had spread to everyone who'd been bitten by the mutated croc people. A scratch or bite from an infected person spread the condition to the next person. It was quickly becoming an epidemic.

The Dark Knight worked feverishly in his lab. He had not found the cure to the mutation despite having samples of DNA from Killer Croc's creatures, from Commissioner Gordon, and from his own wounded shoulder.

Bruce had isolated the strand of DNA that was affected in all three samples. It was an unusual cluster of molecules that attached to healthy cells like a barnacle.

"This isn't like anything I've seen before," Batman said to himself. "Did the Joker or Poison Ivy come up with something new and give it to Killer Croc?"

CLICK! CLICK! The Dark Knight pulled up a computer file. It listed every toxin or poison his Rogues Gallery of super-villains had ever used. There was the Joker's Joker Venom, Poison Ivy's plant toxins, and even Scarecrow's fear formula. All these villains had a talent for creepy chemistry, but this croc plague was beyond even their skills.

What mad genius is was responsible for this outbreak? Batman wondered.

BEEP! BEEP! "Warning: twelve hours remain before transformation is complete," the computer announced.

Batman had set a countdown on the Batcave's main computer as a safety measure. It had taken 24 hours for the first victims to be turned into reptiles. Batman figured it would take that long for him, too. He noticed he was already beginning to lose his ability to concentrate, probably because his human brain was slowly changing into a reptilian one. The computer's reminder helped keep him focused and on track.

"Breaking News from WGTV!" the television blared. Batman jumped. He had forgotten that it was on. "We bring you this update on our top story — The Killer Croc of Doom!"

The bright moving pictures drew his attention. He watched a reporter dressed in a hazmat suit and body armor as she interviewed Killer Croc.

"Mr. Killer Croc, this isn't your normal look," the reporter said. "What happened to you?"

"It was just time for a change," the villain replied. His grin went from ear to ear — at least, what Batman thought were his ears. "I was a tadpole before," he said, leaning close to the camera and baring all of his sharp, white teeth. "But now I'm a T. rex!"

"Reports are coming in that you and your minions are spreading a plague," the reporter continued. "How do you respond to that?"

"Hey, don't blame me!" he said. "It was some guy with a cape and a funny accent who invented it."

*   *   *

At the same time, the mysterious stranger was watching the TV broadcast from his secret headquarters. "Silly Killer Croc," he said to himself. "You have a big mouth — in more ways than one. It's a good thing you're only a small part of my experiment."

HAHAHAHAHAHA!

The shadowy man turned to look at many more monitors. Each screen showed the mutated citizens of Gotham City attacking people all over town. Every scratch and every bite created a new mutant under Killer Croc's control.

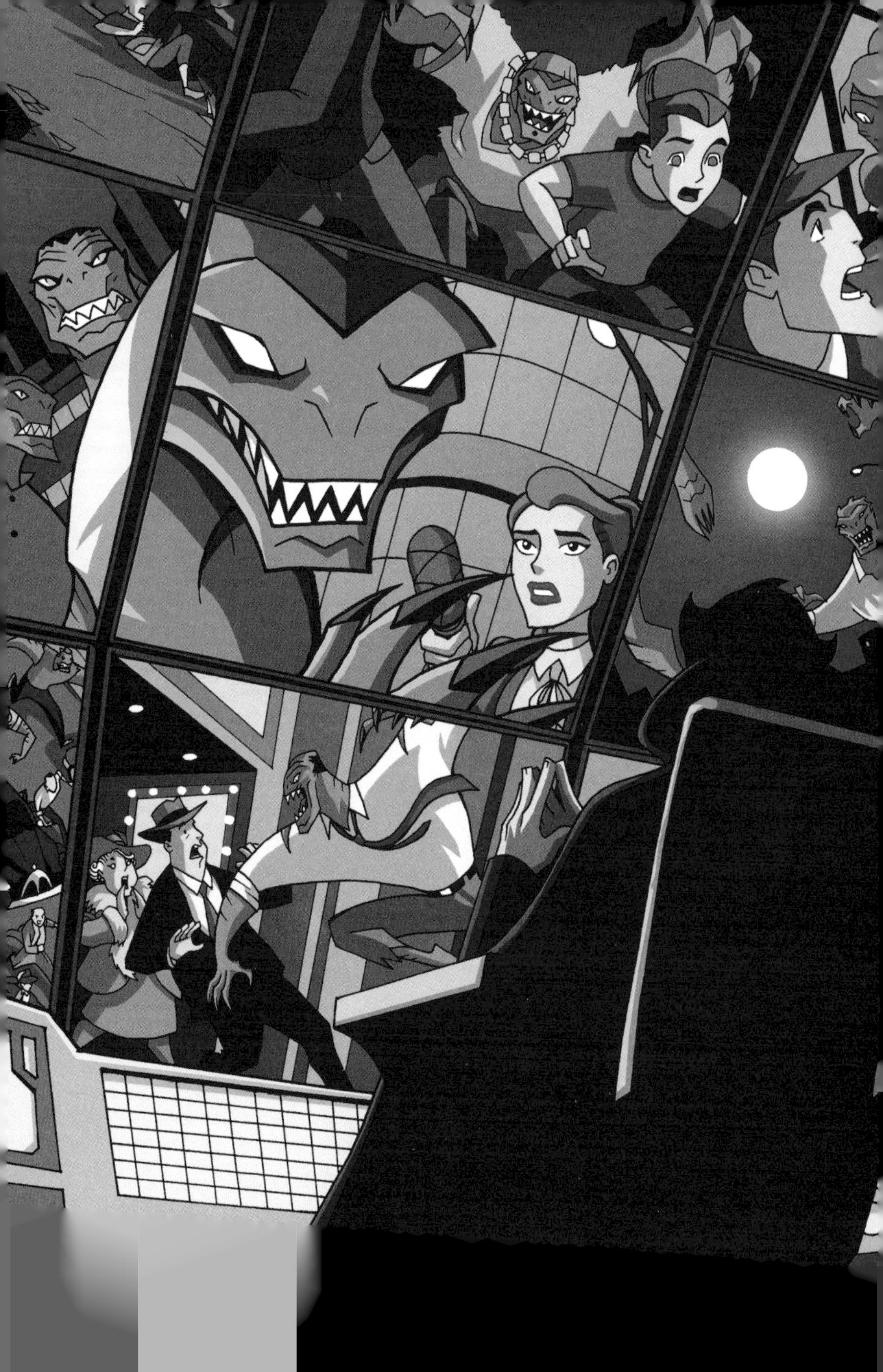

And this was exactly what the man wanted to happen. "Even if the great Dark Knight Detective figures out I am behind this, it will be too late," the man said. "The world will be changed forever. Soon every human on Earth will be turned into one of my servants."

The man turned his glance to another TV screen. This one showed mutants swimming in Gotham Harbor. Police boats had tried to round them up, but the officers on board suffered the same fate as those on land. Once they were wounded, they were infected.

"I love it when a plan comes together," he said. "And now, it's time for phase two."

*   *   *

Back in his Batcave, Batman was watching the same scenes.

A wall of TV monitors showed him what was happening all over the city. The video feed was hooked into every major security camera in Gotham City. As the city's protector, the Dark Knight had access to these video feeds at all times, day or night. But right now the images only made him feel dizzy.

Batman reached to turn off the monitors, but his hand missed the button. *I need to concentrate,* he thought.

Suddenly, another reporter was on the air covering a different story. The criminals of Gotham City were on a crime spree.

"The Joker just staged a smash-and-grab at a jewelry store," the reporter said. She wore a large filter mask to protect her from the villain's dangerous Joker Venom.

"It seems that all the police are busy with the Killer Croc case," the reporter continued. "The crooks of Gotham are taking advantage of their absence."

Batman looked at the monitors. He saw the Joker driving wildly down the street in a getaway car, throwing money out of the windows like a madman.

On another screen, he saw the Penguin waddling down the street with a rare bird sculpture from the Gotham Museum of Art held at his side.

On a third monitor, the Mad Hatter was throwing a brick through the window of a fancy hat boutique.

The motions on the monitors made Batman's head spin. He covered his eyes with his green, scaly hands.

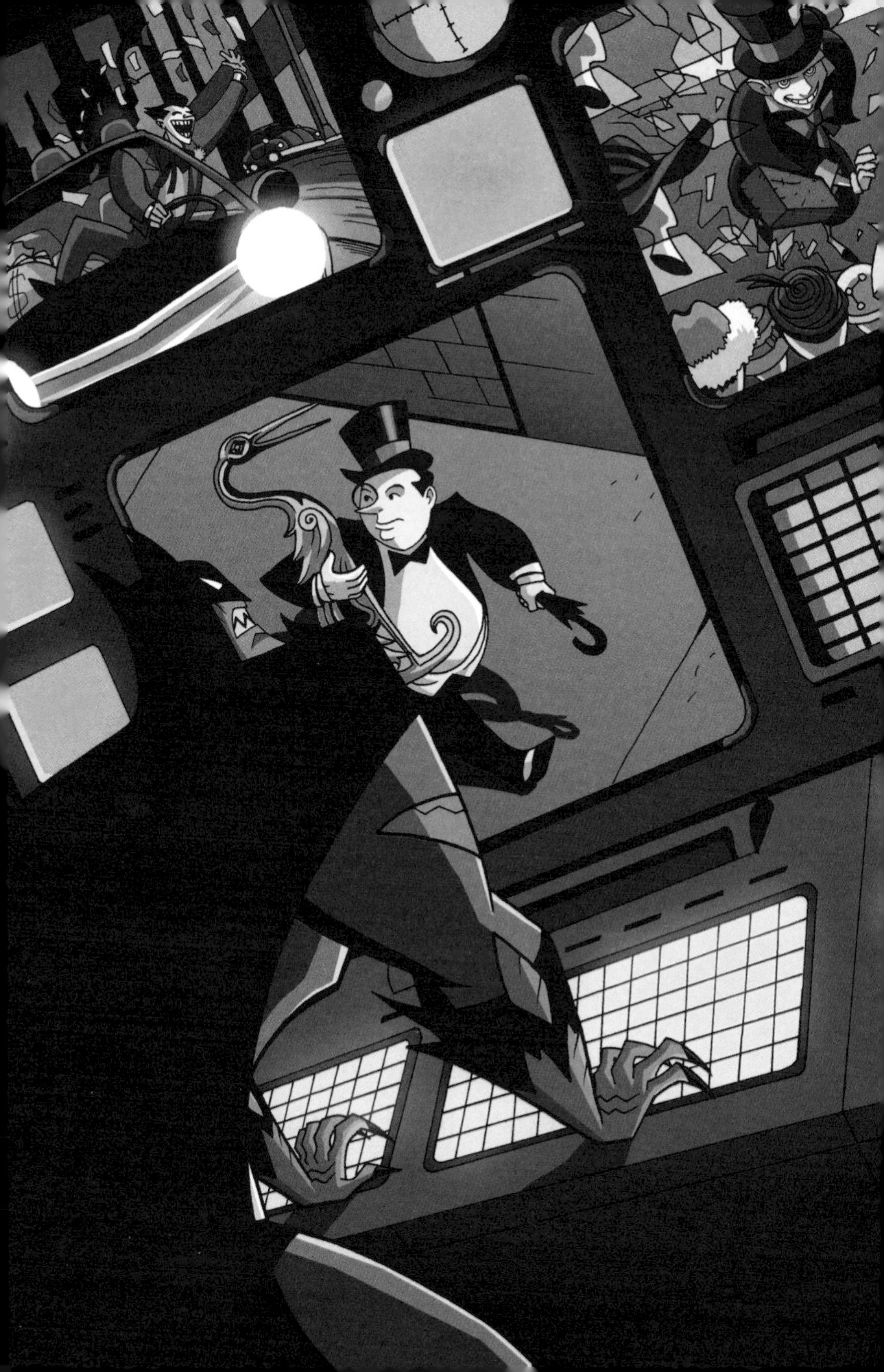

The Dark Knight's palms were too large to wear gloves anymore. His fingers looked more like claws. The change was close to consuming him completely.

Batman tried to turn his mind back to the problem. "Gotham City needs me," said the wounded hero. "I have to find the solution to the croc mutation!"

But even thinking was becoming much more difficult. Primitive thoughts kept invading Batman's head. His body felt hot, then cold, and his bite wound itched constantly. Instinctively, he stretched out his tongue to lick at it like an animal.

"Master Bruce!" Alfred cried.

The sound of his friend and caretaker's voice stopped him. The Dark Knight turned toward the butler.

The intense concern was clear on the older man's face. "Sir, let me change that bandage," Alfred said, composing himself.

"Bandage," Batman repeated. His eyes and voice were focused somewhere distant. "I need a bandage . . . for the wound. The DNA wound."

"Yes, sir," Alfred replied as calmly as he could. He could tell that his friend was beginning to lose his mind. "Let me just remove —"

Suddenly, Batman jumped to his feet. He slapped his clawed hands against the image of the DNA strands on the computer's monitor.

"That's the answer!" the Dark Knight said. "I have to remove it!"

Alfred's eyes went wide with hope.

"Remove what, sir?" the butler asked cautiously.

"The wound to the DNA," Batman replied. "It needs a bandage!"

Alfred knew that his friend wasn't in his normal state of mind, but there seemed to be some sense in the Dark Knight's strange words. He just had to figure out what it was.

"What sort of bandage, sir?" Alfred asked gently. "Shall I fetch it?"

"No first-aid kit has what I need," Batman replied. "But the labs at Wayne Enterprises do."

Batman seemed to be very excited. The adrenaline helped to clear his thoughts, but it also made him look more menacing.

His teeth were bared in a savage smile. His eyes shined like little red lights in the darkness, and slivers of drool dripped from his largest incisors.

"Let's go!" Batman said. His voice sounded more like a growl than words.

Alfred nodded slowly. "Certainly, sir," he said. "But I'll drive."

CHAPTER 3

KILLER OR CURE?

The dark shape of the Batplane landed on the roof of Wayne Enterprises. The aircraft was as silent as its pilot. But the two people who climbed out of the cockpit weren't as quiet.

"It's my plane," Batman growled. "I wanted to fly it!" He was getting more and more irritable because of the transformation.

"Sir, it doesn't matter. We're here," Alfred said. "Where do you wish to go now?"

"Bandage lab," Batman answered with a grunt.

Alfred knew every department of Wayne Enterprises. He had never heard of one called the bandage lab, but he didn't want to point out that fact for fear of angering his volatile partner.

"Lead the way, sir," Alfred suggested.

The pair hurried down the fire stairs from the roof. Batman ran as fast as he could on his clawed feet. His balance was off and he kept banging into the walls, which was the only reason why Alfred was able to keep up with the bigger, faster Batman.

"This floor," Batman said. *THUD!* With a mighty blow, his fist smashed through the fire door. "Oops."

Alfred ran down a hallway behind the staggering super hero. "Please do be more careful, sir," he said. "You don't seem to know your own strength anymore."

Batman let out a deep chuckle. At least, Alfred thought it was a chuckle.

The two men walked down the corridor. At the end of the hall was a metal security door. There was a label on it: NANO LAB.

CLICK! CLICK! Batman tapped the sign gently with a claw and smiled a toothy grin at Alfred. "Bandage lab," the Dark Knight said.

"If you say so, sir," Alfred replied uncertainly.

Of course, being Bruce Wayne, Batman knew the combination of the electronic security lock on the lab's door.

However, Batman did have a little trouble remembering it at first. It took him a couple of tries to get the correct sequence of words.

"Have to hurry," Batman warned Alfred. "My brain is . . . turning."

The door opened into an air lock. On the other side, the rooms were made of glass, steel, and high-impact plastic. Everything was as sterile as a NASA clean room.

"No time for decontamination," Batman mumbled. He pressed an emergency code into the security lock on the inner door. "Will have to take . . . chances."

HISSSSSSSSSSSSSSSSSSSSS!

The door opened. Red warning lights started to flash. Batman froze in his tracks.

The Dark Knight squeezed his eyes shut. The hero held up his arms to block the painfully brilliant lights.

AHHHHHHHHHHH! The loud noises and flashing lights seemed to cause him severe pain.

Alfred dashed over to a control panel and turned off the alarm. The lights stopped flashing.

Batman stood looking around the lab as if he didn't know where he was. He blinked his reptilian eyes a few times. His human brain was fading fast, and the flashing lights had confused him.

"We're in the, uh, bandage lab, sir," Alfred reminded him.

"Yessss," Batman hissed. Even his voice was beginning to change.

Alfred looked around. "What now, sir?" he asked.

"Mussssst program nano-botsssss," came Batman's strange response.

"Show me how, sir," Alfred asked.

"No time . . . to explain," Batman replied. "Musssst do mysssself. While I ssstill have . . . my mind."

The Dark Knight lumbered on crocodile feet to a massive machine that was the core of the nano lab. There was a huge clear plastic dome on top and blocks of computer drives below. A central keyboard controlled it all. Batman placed his fingers on the keys. Then he stopped. His claws had grown too big to type!

ROOOOOOOOOOOOOOAR!

Batman growled in frustration.

The Dark Knight could feel himself losing control. If he did, Gotham City was doomed — and so was he. "Alfred . . . ," Batman whispered. "Come here."

"How may I assist you, sir?" the loyal butler asked.

"Your handssss . . . on keyssss," Batman struggled to say. "My handssss show yours. What to . . . to type."

Alfred placed his hands on the keyboard. Batman put his reptile claws on top of them.

"I understand, sir," Alfred said with a pleasant smile. "My fingers will substitute for yours. It shall make for an interesting duet."

CLICK! CLICK! CLICK! Slowly but surely, they started typing.

Batman's claws pressed on Alfred's fingers to show him the correct keys. The work was slow and awkward. The Dark Knight's brain was growing more and more beast-like.

"Tell me your goal, sir," Alfred suggested. "It might keep you focused."

"Bad molecule on DNA sssssstrands causssed mutation," Batman struggled to say. "Must surgically remove . . . with nano-botssss."

"You've found the antidote?" Alfred asked hopefully.

"Not antidote. Nano bandage," Batman said. "To heal DNA."

BLIP! BLIP!

Miniature mechanical structures started to show up on the computer screen.

These were the ultra-small nano robots that Batman was preparing. They looked like coils of barbed wire.

"Those are very sharp bandages, sir," Alfred observed.

"Cut out bad molecule firsssst," Batman replied. "Then bandage."

The structures on the computer screen took on their final form. Then the core started to manufacture them. A cloud of nano-bots started to grow in the large plastic dome. They looked like a swarm of tiny, silver bees. Batman carefully collected a vial of them in a test tube using the machine's robotic hands.

"Thissss will kill me . . . or cure me," the Dark Knight said. He broke the capsule against his bare hand.

"No, wait!" Alfred protested. But it was too late.

The nano-bots sank into Batman's scaly croc skin. They headed straight for his DNA. The search for the mutated strands did not take long. The bots attacked the infection with microscopic blades that Batman had designed. The mutating molecules were shredded to pieces. Then the nano-bots changed into webs and wrapped themselves around the wounded DNA strands like a bandage.

"It'ssss . . . working," Batman said. "I'm starting to feel like my . . . myself again."

His green scaly skin was fading. His teeth were shrinking back to normal size. His hands and feet no longer looked like claws.

And most importantly, the Dark Knight's mind was clearing. In a matter of seconds, Batman could once again think like a human — not a crocodile.

"I'm going to need a way to spread the nano-bot cure all over Gotham," the Dark Knight said.

Alfred smiled. "I just might have an idea," he said.

*   *   *

Moments later, Batman and Alfred had mounted gas canisters onto the wings of the Batplane. Each container held trillions of nano-bots.

A few minutes later, they sent the plane aloft with a remote control.

VROOOOOOOOOOOOOOM!

Batman controlled the Batplane from the ground as it flew over Gotham. Looking down, he saw that the croc people were everywhere. There were thousands of them.

Batman flew like a crop duster and released the nano gas up and down the streets of the city.

WHOOOOSH!

FWOOOOSH!

The cure kicked in almost instantly. People started changing back to humans before Batman's eyes.

Killer Croc looked up and saw a cloud of nano-bots roll over him. "Awww, gas again?" he complained. "Really?"

Almost instantly, a super-strong web wrapped around him and immobilized him.

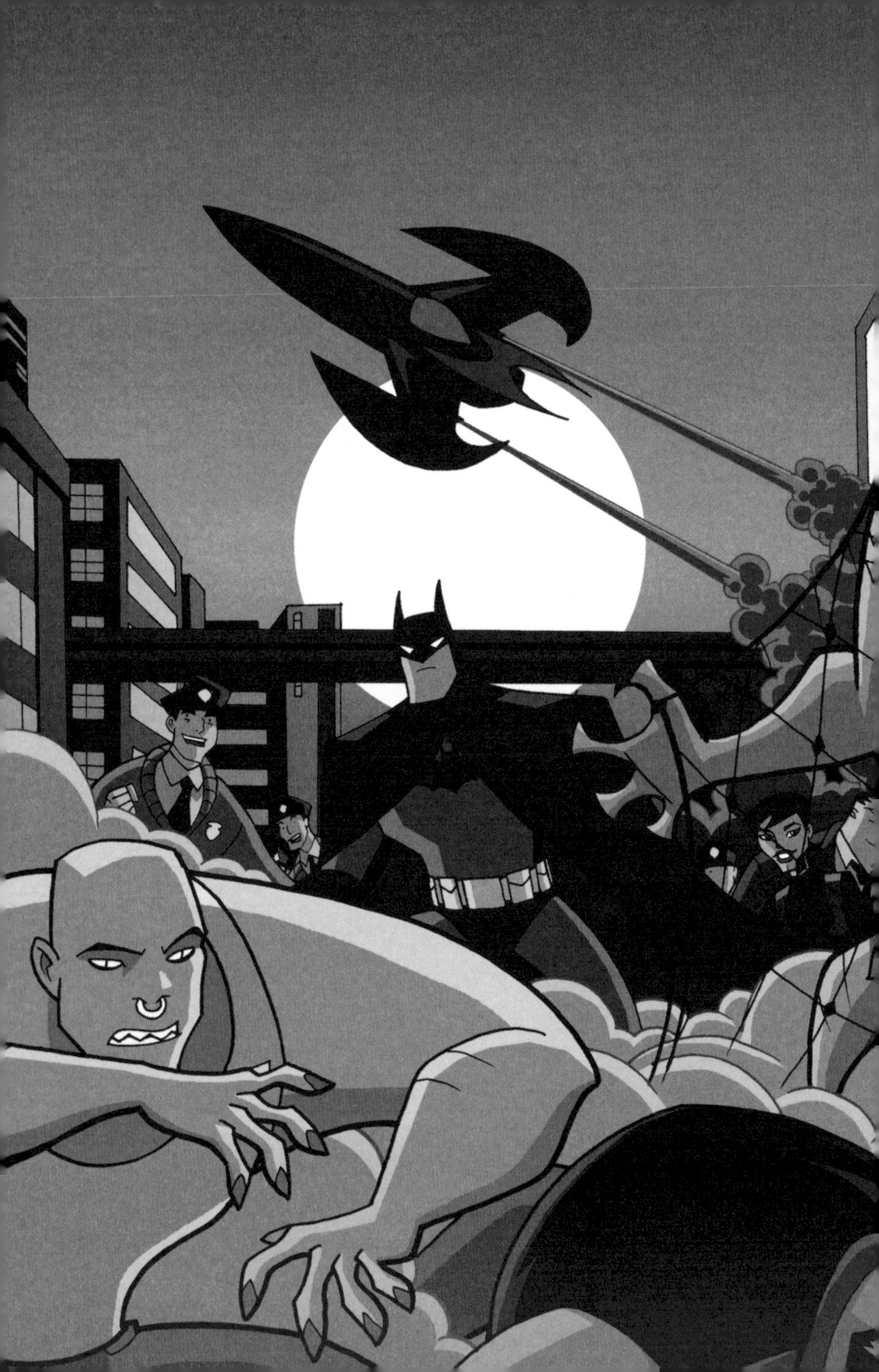

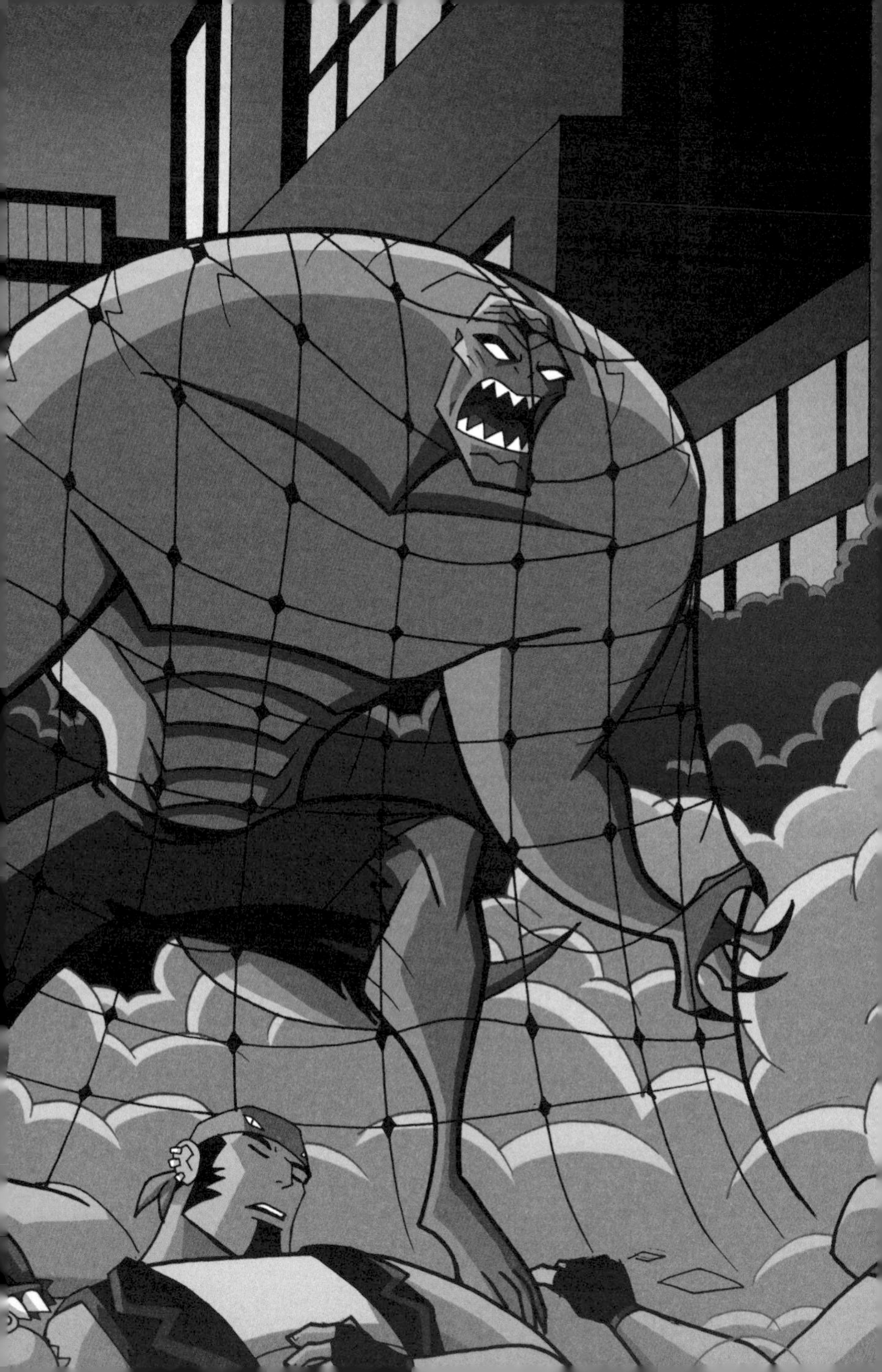

The Dark Knight had simply pressed a button on his remote control, and the Batplane had netted Killer Croc.

FWOOOSH! FWOOOSH!

The angry villain thrashed wildly in his net, but that only made him get more entwined within the super-strong wires.

Commissioner Gordon was waiting for them on the roof of police headquarters. He was back to normal, thanks to Batman and Alfred's nano-bot cure. So were the police officers that took Killer Croc into custody, as well as Killer Croc himself. They happily snapped handcuffs on the villain and marched him downstairs to a jail cell.

"The threat to Gotham is over, thanks to you," Gordon told Batman.

"Not quite," the Dark Knight replied. "Killer Croc wasn't the one behind this epidemic."

"You mean that whoever caused this is still out there?" Gordon asked.

WHIRRRRRR!

A security camera with an attached megaphone on the roof turned its lens toward Batman and Commissioner Gordon. "Once again, the Dark Knight Detective has spoiled my scheme," boomed a voice from the megaphone.

"That voice is very familiar," Batman said. He turned to face the camera. "It belongs to Rā's al Ghūl."

"Correct, Detective," the villainous mastermind said. He watched Batman on the monitors in his secret hideout.

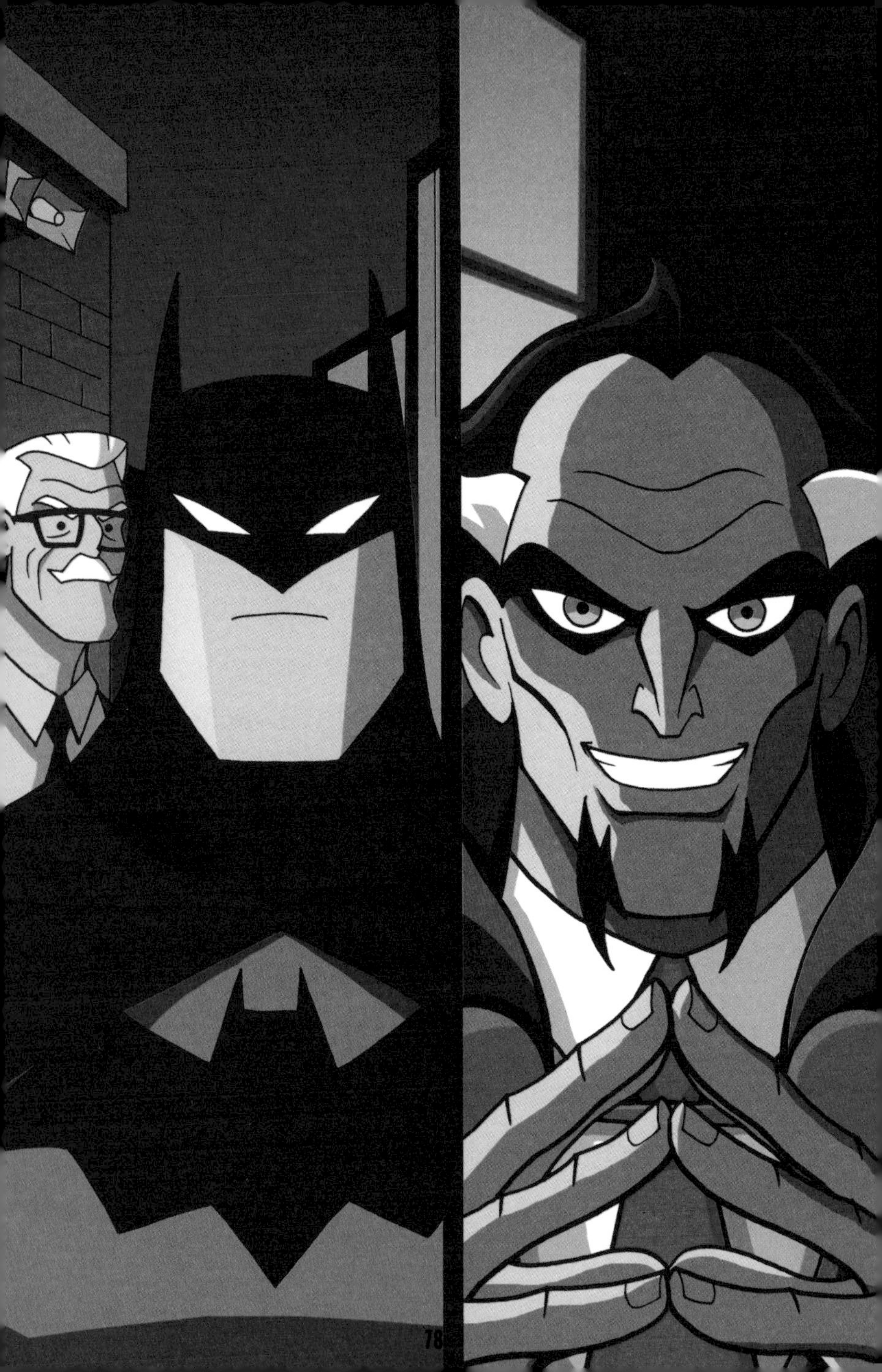

"My experiment has failed because of you," Rā's said.

"Turning people into reptiles is quite a project," said the Dark Knight. "When did you add 'mad scientist' to your list of specialties?"

"I will use any method to cleanse the planet of its human infestation," Rā's replied.

"Humans have as much right to be on the planet as any other creature," Batman said. "They are natural inhabitants, just like the birds and the fish."

"Birds and fish do not strip the world of its minerals or poison the air," Rā's al Ghūl argued.

Batman narrowed his eyes at Rā's al Ghūl.

"While that may be true," Batman said, "it doesn't justify doing what you did."

"A reptilian form of humanoid is better, don't you see?" Rā's said. "It's just too bad you stopped my genetic toxin from making that happen."

"I will always stop you," Batman promised.

"You are a worthy foe, Detective," Rā's said. "I look forward to our next encounter."

"You won't have to wait very long," Batman said. "I've already traced your audio signal to your current location. You're in Tibet. I'll be there in a few hours to arrest you."

Rā's al Ghūl gritted his teeth.

But then, slowly, Rā's al Ghūl's angry grin slowly turned into a smile. "Ah, you truly are the World's Greatest Detective," Rā's praised his foe.

CLICK! Then the transmission ended. "That's my specialty," Batman said.

KILLER CROC

REAL NAME:
Waylon Jones

OCCUPATION:
Professional Criminal

BASE:
Gotham City's Sewers

HEIGHT:
7 feet 5 inches

WEIGHT:
686 pounds

EYES:
Red

HAIR:
None

Waylon Jones was born with a rare disease that made his skin scaly and green. Seen as a monster wherever he went, he decided to use his fearsome appearance to frighten his opponents as a professional wrestler. "Killer Croc" easily muscled his way through the ranks to become champion. Croc soon began to realize just how strong he really was and decided to use that strength to his advantage. Before long, Killer Croc was feared throughout the criminal underworld — and at the top of the most wanted list.

- Croc has a skin disease called "epidermolytic hyperkeratosis." It has made his skin tough and scaly, protecting him from knives and bullets. It also makes him look like a crocodile.

- Croc once asked a scientist to cure him of his crocodile-like disease. When the treatment failed, he lost his temper and swallowed the scientist whole!

- With his razor-sharp claws and jagged teeth, Killer Croc is a dangerous super-villain. He has been known to give in to animal-like rages, making him extremely unpredictable and deadly.

- Kliller Croc has super-speed, super-strength, and fast healing powers. He can even regrow lost limbs, making it extremely difficult to put this vile villain down for the count.

BIOGRAPHIES

LAURIE S. SUTTON has read comics since she was a kid. She grew up to become an editor for Marvel, DC Comics, Starblaze, and Tekno Comics. She has written *Adam Strange* for DC, *Star Trek: Voyager* for Marvel, plus *Star Trek: Deep Space Nine* and *Witch Hunter* for Malibu Comics. There are long boxes of comics in her closet where there should be clothing and shoes. Laurie has lived all over the world, and currently resides in Florida.

LUCIANO VECCHIO was born in 1982 and currently lives in Buenos Aires, Argentina. With experience in illustration, animation and comics, his works have been published in the US, Spain, UK, France, and Argentina. Credits include *Ben 10* (DC Comics), *Cruel Thing* (Norma), *Unseen Tribe* (Zuda Comics), and *Sentinels* (Drumfish Productions).

GLOSSARY

decontamination (dee-kuhn-tam-uh-NAY-shuhn)—the process of removing harmful substances from something or someplace

deformed (di-FORMD)—twisted, bent, or disfigured

despised (di-SPIZED)—if someone is despised, they are greatly disliked

insecure (in-si-KYOOR)—anxious and not confident

minion (MIN-yuhn)—a person who obediently serves or works for a powerful person or organization

mutation (myoo-TAY-shuhn)—a change in genetic structure

penetrate (PEN-uh-trate)—to break through or go inside something

primitive (PRIM-uh-tiv)—very simple or crude, or to do with an early stage of development

shivering (SHIV-ur-ing)—shaking with cold or fear

sinister (SIN-uh-stur)—seeming evil and threatening

vulnerable (VUHL-nur-uh-buhl)—at risk of being harmed, or able to be harmed

DISCUSSION QUESTIONS

1. Alfred and Batman make a great team. Who do you work well with? Why? Talk about partners.

2. Killer Croc starts a gang. Why are gangs often bad? Can they ever be good? Talk about gangs.

3. This book has ten illustrations. Which one is your favorite? Why?

WRITING PROMPTS

1. In the end of this book, Batman discovers that Rā's Al Ghūl was behind everything. What happens next in this story? Does Batman manage to catch the villain? Write another chapter to this book.

2. Batman is slower and weaker than Killer Croc, but he managed to defeat the super-villain anyway. What are some advantages Batman has over Killer Croc? Write about them.

3. Killer Croc becomes bigger, stronger, and faster than ever before. Imagine yourself as a monster. What would you look like? What would your special abilities be? Write about it, then draw a picture of your monstrous self.

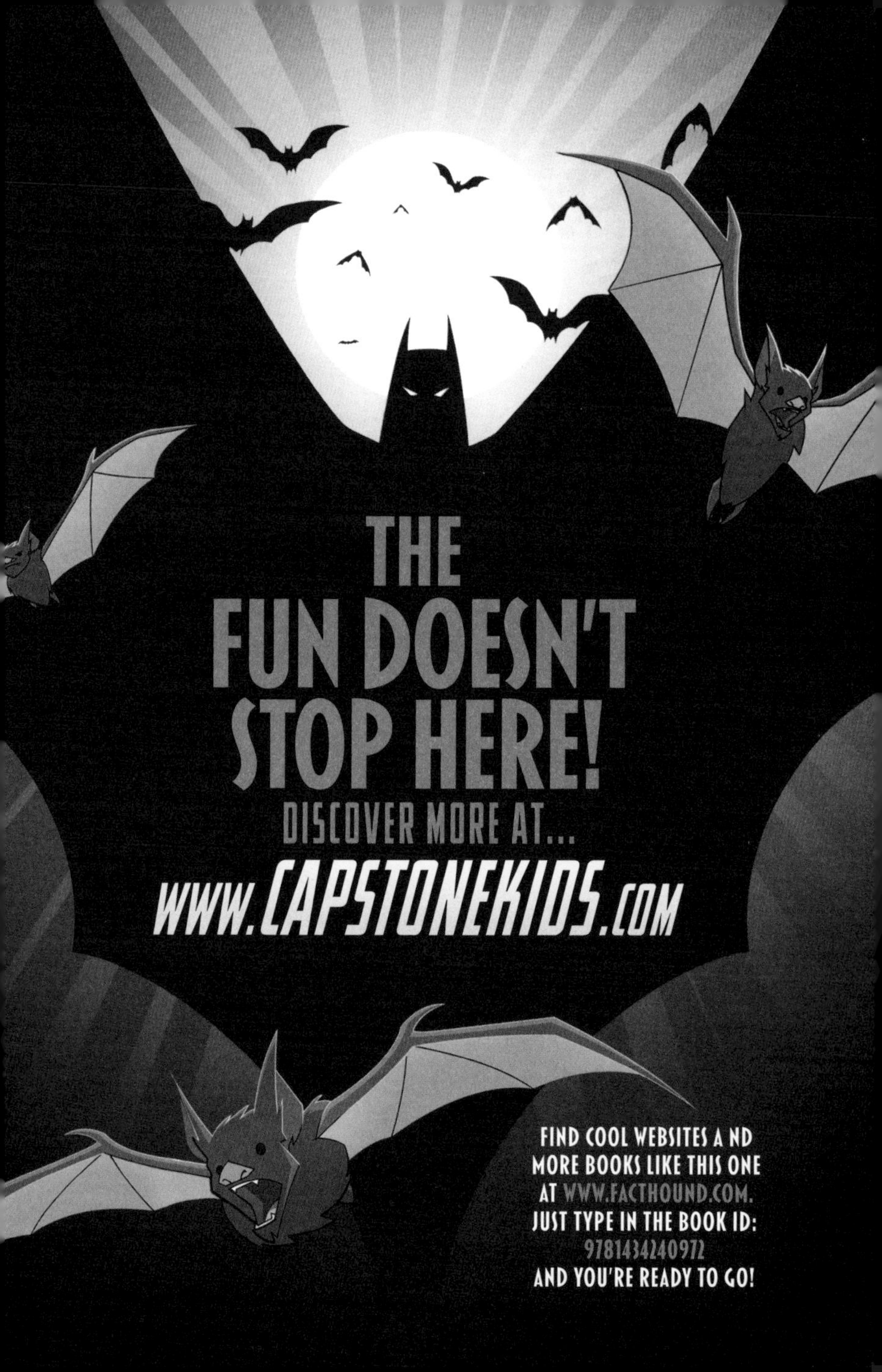
THE
FUN DOESN'T
STOP HERE!
DISCOVER MORE AT...
WWW.CAPSTONEKIDS.COM
FIND COOL WEBSITES A ND
MORE BOOKS LIKE THIS ONE
AT WWW.FACTHOUND.COM.
JUST TYPE IN THE BOOK ID:
9781434240972
AND YOU'RE READY TO GO!

LOOK FOR MORE THE DARK KNIGHT™

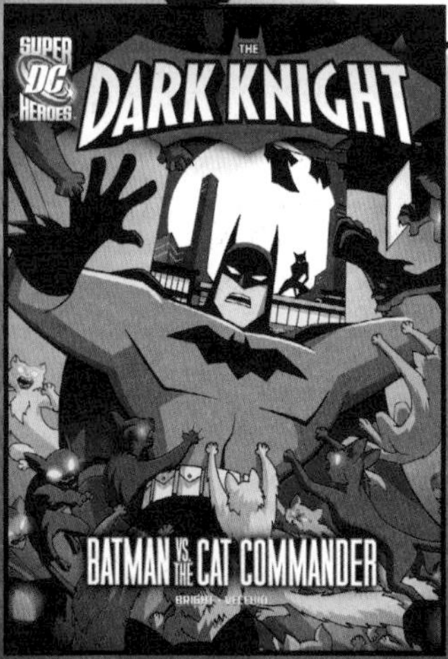
SUPER DC HEROES
THE DARK KNIGHT
BATMAN VS. THE CAT COMMANDER
BRIGHT · VECCHIO

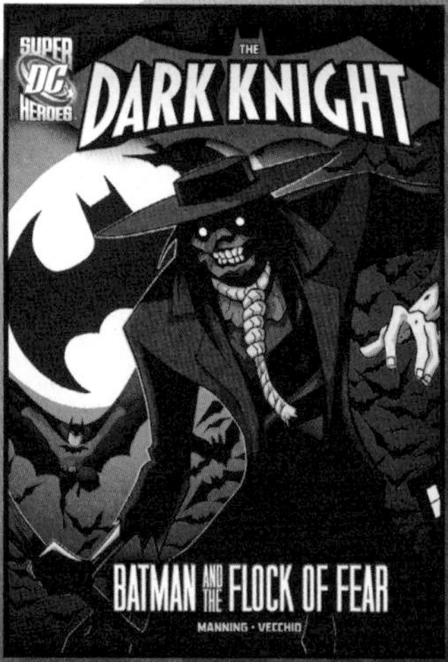
SUPER DC HEROES
THE DARK KNIGHT
BATMAN AND THE FLOCK OF FEAR
MANNING · VECCHIO

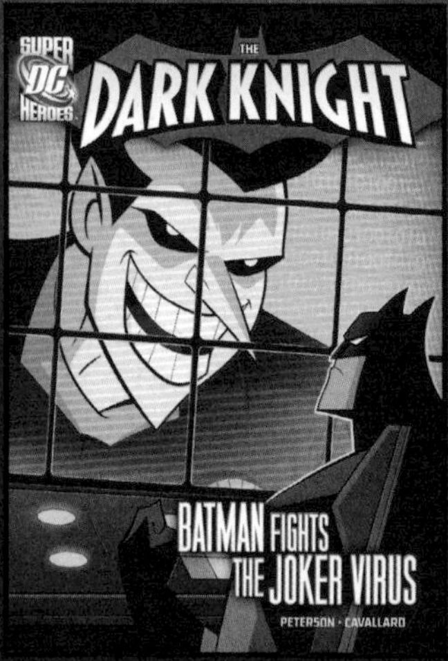
SUPER DC HEROES
THE DARK KNIGHT
BATMAN FIGHTS THE JOKER VIRUS
PETERSON · CAVALLARO

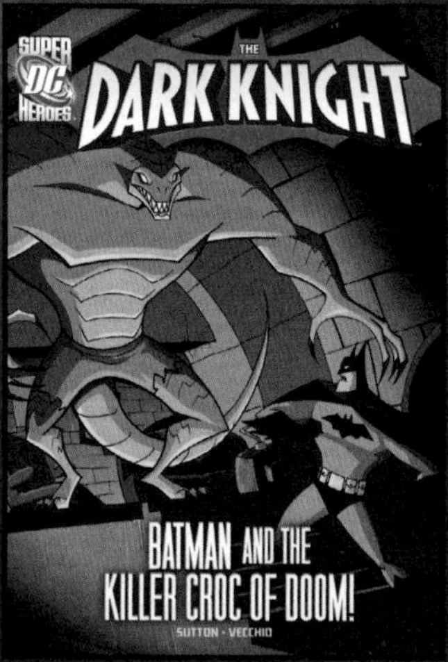
SUPER DC HEROES
THE DARK KNIGHT
BATMAN AND THE KILLER CROC OF DOOM!
SUTTON · VECCHIO